Alice Savage

THE YELLOW HOUSE ON SUMMER STREET

Alice Savage grew up in a theatrical family and began writing plays and stories in the fifth grade. As an English teacher of adult learners, she combines creative writing with a deep awareness of language to illuminate the worlds of immigrants and cultural explorers. She credits her multicultural family as inspiration. An author on many course books for Oxford University Press, Cambridge University Press, Pearson, and others, Alice has presented widely on the role of drama in language learning. She has published several award-winning one-act plays. Her dramatic fiction shows what happens when characters address challenges for which they may or may not be prepared. Alice lives and teaches in Houston, Texas.

First published by Gemma in 2024.

www.gemmamedia.org

Printed in the United States of America

978-1-956476-33-0

Library of Congress Cataloging-in Publication Data available.

Cover by Laura Shaw Design

Named after the brightest star in the Northern Crown, Gemma is a nonprofit organization that helps new readers acquire English language literacy skills with relevant, engaging books, eBooks, and audiobooks. Always original, never adapted, these stories introduce adults and young adults to the life-changing power of reading.

GEMMA

Open Door

To my ever-expanding
multicultural family

TABLE OF CONTENTS

1. Houston

Joe parks in front of a small yellow house. He takes a deep breath and turns to his wife, Brita. "Are you sure about this?"

Brita smiles. "I don't know, Joe. Let's ask the kids." She turns to the back seat where Kyle, who is five, and Ethan, two and a half, are sitting. "Your dad is worried. He thinks maybe we bought the wrong house. What do you think? Should we give it back?"

"No!" They both shout. They do not like looking at houses. They like this house. The yard is big. It goes all the way around the house, and there are trees.

"Okay, okay." Joe turns off the car and opens the door. The movers are already in the driveway. Before he gets out, Brita puts her hand on his arm.

"This is the right house, Joe." She smiles. "We're going to raise our kids here."

"I know," Joe says. "I just worry. I don't want anything to go wrong."

Joe's real name is Yusef. He is from Syria, but he has been in the US a long time, and people call him Joe. Joe is able to change his name, but he cannot stop worrying. He is always a little more nervous than his American wife.

Joe watches Brita take the boys into the yard. Then she walks over to three movers standing next to their truck. He likes Brita's confidence. If she says everything is going to be fine, maybe it will be.

Joe moves boxes out of the car while

Brita unlocks the door and directs the movers. The boys follow a white cat to the backyard. They do not return, so Joe goes to check on them. He finds them under a tree. They are planning to build a tree house.

Joe says, "Okay. Which tree?"

Kyle starts looking at the different trees. Ethan looks up and laughs. He points to a pair of squirrels in one of the trees. The little animals are chasing each other and making noise.

"Squirrels!" says Joe.

"Quir!" says Ethan.

Joe does not know it, but behind the tree and the squirrels, someone is watching them. There is a big house next door. An old woman is looking out her upstairs window. She frowns. She does not like little boys, and the man seems foreign.

The old woman turns to a small dog. "Tilly," she says. "This can't be good."

The dog looks at the woman with big brown eyes. The old woman shakes her head. "No, it's not good." She turns back to the window. "If those boys make trouble, they'll be sorry."

Suddenly, Ethan looks up. He sees the woman, and he smiles. The woman does not smile back. She leaves the window.

Joe sees Ethan's smile. He looks at the window, but he does not see anyone. Joe looks at Ethan. Ethan runs away. Then he falls. Joe runs after him. He picks up his crying son and holds him.

The movers finish their work, and

Brita pays them. Then she brings drinks for Joe and the boys. The family sits on the porch. Joe and Kyle tell her about their plans for the tree house. Little Ethan says, "Quir."

"Quir?" asks Brita.

"Squirrels," says Joe. "The trees are full of squirrels."

"Fun!" says Brita. "I like this house."

"Me, too," says Kyle. "But I miss my friends."

"You'll make new friends," says Brita.

"I hope so," says Kyle.

Kyle does not know it, but someone is listening. Down the street, a boy named Teddy is in front of a white house with blue windows. Teddy hears Kyle's voice. He runs inside and tells his mother. "There's a boy."

5

Dolores looks out the window. "A boy? Where?"

"Down the street, in the yellow house."

"That's great, Teddy! Maybe you can make a new friend."

"Maybe," says Teddy. "Do you think he likes trucks or trains?"

"I don't know. Does it matter?"

"I guess not," says Teddy. "But I have both, just in case."

"Wonderful," says Dolores. "I can't wait to meet them!"

Other neighbors are also watching the movers. They ask themselves the same question. What will this new family bring to Summer Street?

2. Jordan

On a crowded street in Ahman, Jordan, it is night. Light shines from the windows of a small café. Three young men are sitting around a table.

Rashid finishes his tea and lights a cigarette. "We can't go back to Syria," he says.

"I have to," says Nabil. "My mom won't leave Aleppo. She wants to stay in the house."

"Do you know that for sure?"

"I can't reach her, but that's the last thing she said."

"Don't do it. Aleppo is a pile of rocks," says Amir.

"She's got my sister there, too," says Nabil.

"I'll go with you," says Rashid.

"You can't. They'll put you in the army," Nabil says.

"And you! They'll put you in the army, too."

"No one can go," says Amir. He puts some money on the table with his one good hand, "especially you, Rashid."

"Why me?"

"You're very good at getting into trouble."

"Is that a compliment?" asks Rashid.

"It's a fact," says Amir.

Rashid laughs. "I don't look for trouble."

"I'm glad to hear that," says Amir. "If

we want to help our families, we need to get to Germany or Sweden. We need to go to university."

"My mom still thinks I can get into college in the US," Rashid laughs. "Talk about crazy ideas." He puts out his cigarette. "She's talking to my uncle in Texas."

"Texas? Are you kidding?" Nabil takes one of Rashid's cigarettes.

"I know. Crazy, huh? He just bought a house, so she thinks he has room."

"Well, your mom usually gets what she wants," says Nabil. "She got us into the British Academy in Aleppo."

"My mother's Aleppo connections are not going to help in Houston."

"If I know your mother, you better

start learning Texan," Nabil says. "It's very different from your British school English."

Rashid laughs, "It's your English, too!"

"Thanks to your mom!" Nabil picks up his glass of tea. It is cold now, but he drinks it anyway. "In Texas, people put ice in their tea," he says, lighting his cigarette.

"No way," says Amir.

"They do," says Rashid.

"Well, that's weird, but you should still go if you can," says Amir. "I would."

"Would you really want to go to Texas?"

"Yes, in a minute." Amir laughs. "I look good in a cowboy hat."

Suddenly, Amir stops. He looks over

Rashid's shoulder, and his voice changes. "Don't look now, but someone is watching us."

"Does he have a beard?" asks Rashid. He does not turn around. Neither does Nabil.

"Yes."

"Red hat?"

"Yes."

"Well, then. It's been nice talking, but I better go." Rashid gets up. "I'll see you guys tomorrow." Rashid starts walking quickly down the street in the other direction. As soon as he is out of the light, Rashid runs. The man in the red hat starts running after him. Nabil sticks out his leg. The man falls. He gets up angrily.

"Sorry. I didn't see you," Nabil says.

The man in the red hat gets up. He stares at Nabil. "You're next," he says. Then he turns and runs after Rashid.

"Nice hat," Nabil calls after him.

"Who was that?" Amir asks.

"I don't know. But I think I just did Rashid a favor."

Amir looks down the dark street. "What did Rashid do?"

Nabil shrugs, "Probably stopped that guy from cheating a refugee."

"Rashid's 'nice, safe job' at the refugee camp is not so safe, is it?"

"Nope," says Nabil. "We've got to get Rashid out of here."

Amir takes a deep breath, "So what's the plan?"

"We have to separate." Nabil is quiet

for a moment. He looks away. His eyes fill with tears. "I can't stay here."

"What's Rashid supposed to do if you leave?" Amir finally asks. "Who's going to take care of him?"

"You will."

"Me?" Amir sits back in his chair. "With one hand and a bad leg?"

"You have a point," says Nabil looking at Amir's empty shirt sleeve. "But you can help him in other ways. Get him to leave. Help his mom get him into university in Texas."

Amir sighs and nods. "Will we see you again?"

"God willing," says Nabil. "Do you need help getting home?"

"No, I can manage." Amir points to his stick.

They stand. Nabil hugs his friend and disappears into the night.

Amir looks around, but no one is following him. He picks up his stick and walks to the small apartment he shares with his family. *Nabil is right*, Amir thinks. *Rashid must go to Texas*.

3. The Call

On Saturday morning, Brita and Joe drink coffee on the porch. Ethan puts rocks in Kyle's truck, and Kyle empties it on the grass. Joe does not want rocks in the grass, but he does not say anything.

Brita tells Joe about the new neighbors. She met the girl across the street. "Her name is Olivia. She lives with her mother and three cats. She works in a hair salon on Nineteenth Street, and she's saving money for college."

"How do you get all this information?" Joe asks.

Brita smiles, "I like meeting people."

"And they like meeting you," says Joe.

"My next goal is the family two

houses down. I saw a little boy in the yard. I think he's about Kyle's age. Maybe Kyle can make a friend before school starts."

Joe looks at Brita, "That's strange to me. When I was a kid, we made our own friends."

"I did that too," says Brita. "But it's different now. Kids have playdates."

"I know. That's so weird," says Joe. "You're Kyle's social manager, and he's only five."

"We're living in a different world," says Brita. She waves to an old woman walking her dog. "That's Miss Polly," she says. The old woman looks quickly at Joe and Brita, but she does not wave back.

"She lives in the big house next door," says Brita.

"Miss Polly doesn't seem very friendly," says Joe.

"She's not," says Brita cheerfully, "but I'm going to change that. Her dog's name is Tilly. I'm going to start with the dog. Owners like it when you talk to their dog."

Joe looks at his wife. "Do dogs have playdates, too?"

"I think they do," Brita laughs.

Just then, Joe's phone lights up, and he looks down. "It's from Jordan."

"You'd better answer," Brita sits back and watches while Joe answers the phone. He speaks in Arabic. Then he listens. He stands up. He goes down the porch steps and walks along the fence.

Miss Polly walks by going the other direction. She hears Arabic. She stops

17

and looks at Joe. Then she pulls her dog to walk faster.

Brita does not see Miss Polly pull her dog away. She is watching Joe. Brita knows that a call from Joe's relatives can be good. It can also mean bad news. She remembers a day when Joe got a terrible call. It was a Sunday afternoon. They were eating lunch. Joe picked up the phone with a smile, and then his face went white.

His brother was dead.

Caleb was working at a hospital in Syria. A bomb exploded. It killed Caleb along with 132 other doctors, nurses, and patients. Suddenly, Caleb's wife, son, and daughter were alone.

Now, Brita watches Joe's face carefully. He does not seem upset, but her heart is beating a little faster. Joe seems to be asking questions. Finally, he ends the call.

Brita looks at Joe, "What is it?"

Joe looks at Brita. "That was my nephew."

"Which one?"

"Caleb's son."

"Caleb is your brother who died?"

"Yes, his son's name is Rashid."

"Oh right, you've told me about Rashid, the wild one."

Joe looks away. "I shouldn't have said that. He's a good kid. He's just … he has a lot of energy."

"What is it? Is Rashid in trouble?"

"I don't think so. In fact, it could be a good thing."

"What is it?"

"He wants to study here."

"Oh? I thought he was going to Germany."

"His mother wants him to come here."

"And live with us?" Brita understands now.

Joe looks at his two boys playing in the yard. The squirrels are running up and down the trees. The sky is a calm blue above them. Joe does not want to think about the Syrian war, but he cannot escape it, even on this quiet street.

Joe looks at his wife. "I didn't promise anything. I told them we'd discuss it."

"Of course, he can come," says Brita. "Family is important, and we need to help."

"Are you sure?" Joe says. "He can live with us?"

"Yes. Of course!"

"Thank you," says Joe, "But before you say 'yes,' you should think carefully. It might mean a big change."

"I don't need to think about it. He is family, and family is always welcome."

4. Friends

Olivia gets up late on Saturday morning. She looks out the window. Kyle and Ethan are playing in the yard outside the yellow house. She is disappointed because they are so young. Still, the mom is nice, and the boys are cute.

She goes downstairs and finds a note from her mother. "Feed the cats and yourself today. I have to stay late." Olivia's cats are pushing against her legs. They are hungry, but she is not. She puts down some food and then walks to her job on Nineteenth Street.

The salon is small but busy. Olivia is only eighteen, but she is good at cutting hair. Many customers are neighbors. She knows their names and all about their lives. Sometimes people just come in to talk.

Today, the first two customers are Brita and Ethan.

"Hello, Olivia," says Brita. "Remember us?"

"Of course, I'm going to cut Ethan's hair today!"

"It's his first haircut," says Brita. "I love his hair, but it's hard to take care of."

"He does have nice hair," says Olivia. "Are you sure?"

"Yes," says Brita.

"No," says Ethan. He shakes his head.

"Come here, Ethan!" Brita picks him up.

Olivia puts some books on the chair.

Brita helps Ethan sit on the books. He does not smile. He turns around to climb down. Brita grabs him and holds him.

"What kind of haircut do you want, Ethan?" Olivia asks.

Ethan does not speak. He puts his face in Brita's shoulder.

"It's okay, Ethan," Brita puts him back in the chair. "Sit quietly, and Miss Olivia can do it fast."

Oliva puts water on Ethan's hair.

"Ethan likes your cats," says Brita.

Olivia begins to cut. "You can visit them."

Ethan nods.

"Ooops! Don't do that!" Olivia accidentally cuts Ethan's ear.

"Ouch!" says Ethan.

"Sorry," Olivia says.

"I want to go home!" Ethan yells. "It hurts!"

Olivia looks at Brita. Ethan's hair is short on one side and long on the other.

At that moment, the door opens, and a woman comes in the shop. She has a friendly face and long dark hair. "Hello, Olivia!"

"Hi, Dolores," says Olivia. "What's up?"

"Oh, not much," says Dolores. "I just wanted to make an appointment." She looks at Ethan. "I want a haircut like that," she says. Brita laughs, but Ethan is crying now. He reaches for his mother, and Brita picks him up.

Olivia turns to Brita. "What do you want to do?"

"We need to finish this haircut," Brita says. "You have to be still, Ethan."

Dolores looks at Ethan and smiles. Then she takes some pink paper out of her purse. "Do you like birds?" she asks.

"Quir," says Ethan.

Dolores nods. "I don't know how to make a squirrel, but I can make a bird. Do you want to see?"

Ethan nods.

"I'll make you a bird, but you have to watch carefully," says Dolores. She moves in front of Ethan and begins folding the pink paper. Ethan watches while Olivia moves to the other side. She quickly cuts Ethan's hair.

"There!" Dolores says.

Now, Ethan has short hair on both

sides, and Brita is happy. "You look great, Ethan!" Then she turns to Dolores. "Thank you."

"I'm happy to help. A hair salon is a dangerous place." Dolores hands Ethan the small pink bird. Ethan flies it through the air. The paper wings go up and down.

Brita smiles. "I'm Brita. We just moved onto Summer Street."

"I know," says Dolores. "I'm Dolores."

Brita looks confused.

"My son told me about you," Dolores says. "He watches you when you go for walks, and he gave me a full report."

"Oh, that's so funny because Kyle and I often talk about the boy down the street."

"Teddy, his name is Teddy."

"I'd love to get them together," says Brita.

"Well, why don't you come over? We're home this afternoon, and I just made a cake. Do you like tres leches?"

"Yes," says Brita. She has never eaten a tres leches cake, but that is not important. Brita has already decided. Dolores will be her friend.

"You'll love it. It's my mother's recipe from Mexico."

"That sounds wonderful," says Brita. "We'll have lunch, and then I can bring Kyle over." She opens the door, still talking.

"I'll walk with you," says Dolores.

Brita forgets to pay for Ethan's haircut, and Dolores forgets to make the appointment. They walk out of the shop and into the sunshine.

Olivia sighs and begins to clean up Ethan's hair. She will catch up with them later.

5. One Suitcase

On Sunday, Joe and the boys make pancakes for breakfast. Brita gets up late and joins them at the table. Kyle is telling Joe about Teddy.

"He has four fire trucks!" says Kyle.

Brita tells Joe about the playdate. The boys turned on the water and made a big mess. "They were very dirty," Brita says. "But Dolores said it's okay for boys to get dirty, and I agree."

"I don't think you can stop them," says Joe.

"As long as they are having fun," says Brita. "At least they weren't playing with real fire."

"It sounds like you've both made a new friend," says Joe.

"There's a father, but he was at work. We'll meet him soon," Brita says.

Next, Joe and Brita move Kyle's things into Ethan's bedroom. Rashid is coming later, and he will sleep in Kyle's room. Kyle is not happy. He watches his parents move his trains into the new bedroom.

"Ethan messes up my trains!" he says.

"I know," says Brita. "But when family comes, we all have to do our part."

"Is Ethan doing his part?"

"Ethan is sharing his room with you."

"Then it's just like before, when we were in the apartment."

Brita sighs. "I know you like having your own room, but you have good things. You have a big yard and a new friend."

"And we'll build a tree house for you," Joe says. He does not know how to build a tree house, but he will try.

When they finish, Joe and Kyle go to the airport. Joe puts Kyle into the back seat. He gets in and starts the car. Then, he gets out and comes back in the house.

"Forgot my phone," he tells Brita.

"I know." Brita hands him his phone. "Are you nervous?"

"What do you think?" says Joe.

"You're nervous," says Brita. "You're worried about Rashid."

"War does things to people," says Joe.

"We've been through all this, Joe. Let's just make him feel welcome."

Joe kisses Brita. "Thank you," he says. "I love you for that."

Joe gets back in the car, and they drive away.

Brita's right, Joe thinks as he gets on the freeway. Rashid will need help. If Brita can help with the feelings, Joe can help with the immigration paperwork.

Kyle is also thinking. "Does Rashid like kids?" he asks.

"Of course, he likes kids," says Joe. "He's fun. You'll see."

At the airport, they go to the international arrivals. Many people are watching two big doors. Passengers come out with large suitcases. An airline worker pushes an old woman in a wheelchair. A black scarf covers her hair. Her daughter and grandchildren run up. They give her flowers, and she cries.

Finally, Joe points to a thin young man with one small suitcase. He has thick black hair and large dark eyes. Sunglasses are pushed up on his head.

"There he is," says Joe.

Rashid sees Joe. He comes over, and they hug. Then they start talking in Arabic.

Joe remembers Kyle, and he changes to English. "Rashid, this is Kyle, my son."

Rashid smiles at Kyle. He holds out his hand. "Hello, Kyle." Kyle looks at his father. Joe nods, and they shake hands.

Rashid says something in Arabic, and they laugh.

"What?" asks Kyle.

"Rashid says you look like he did when he was little," says Joe.

Kyle says, "I'm not little. I'm five, and I'll be six in November."

Rashid gets down on his knees. Now he is the same height as Kyle. "Almost six? I had fun when I was six. Do you like soccer?"

"Yes," says Kyle.

"Maybe we can kick the ball around some time."

Kyle nods. Rashid gets up, and they continue walking. Kyle holds his father's hand and listens to the Arabic. His father sounds happy in this strange language. He talks fast, and he laughs more.

When they arrive at the yellow house, Brita comes outside to say hello. Rashid is polite. "Thank you for having me!" he says in English.

"It's no trouble," says Brita.

"Are you sure?" asks Rashid.

"It's no trouble at all," says Brita. "Your room is ready."

Rashid puts his hand over his heart and nods his head. "Thank you."

Brita smiles. "I'll check on dinner. I hope you like chicken."

"I love chicken," says Rashid.

"Good," she says and takes the boys inside. They go to the window.

"He seems fine to me," Brita says

looking out. "I don't know why your father is so worried."

Rashid is still talking to Joe. Now he has Kyle's soccer ball between his feet, and he starts to play with it. He kicks it, and the ball goes into the street. A dark blue car turns the corner. Rashid does not see it, and he runs after the ball. The car brakes suddenly. Rashid looks up, surprised. The driver yells at him out the window.

Joe is angry now. "What is your problem?" he yells back at the driver. "No one's hurt!" The driver speeds away.

"That was interesting," says Brita.

Across the street, Olivia hears shouting and goes to the window. She sees Rashid. He is standing on the sidewalk with the ball under his arm. Olivia opens the window and takes a photo. Rashid sees movement in the window. He looks up at Olivia. He smiles and shrugs. Olivia is surprised. She smiles back.

Joe touches Rashid's arm. Rashid turns and follows Joe back to the yard. They take a suitcase out of the car. The door to the house opens, and Rashid goes inside.

Olivia texts the photo of Rashid to her friend Keiko. She writes "I think my summer just got a lot more interesting."

6. Tilly

It is late at night. Miss Polly cannot sleep. She gets up and drinks some water. She picks up a book and reads.

When the sun comes up, her eyes hurt. She hears noise from the yellow house. She looks out the window and sees Teddy. He is standing under a big tree and looking up. A young man and another boy are in the tree.

Miss Polly shakes her head at Tilly. She gets up and makes tea. She is just starting breakfast when she hears shouting.

Miss Polly goes to the window. Brita is standing under the tree next to Teddy.

"Kyle?" she calls up into the tree.

"Look mom! I'm up here!" he shouts.

"How did you get up there?" Brita sounds nervous.

"Rashid helped me. I can see inside my bedroom!" Kyle says.

"It's nice you can see in your bedroom, honey. But can you come down?" Brita says.

"Why?" asks Kyle.

Brita looks at Rashid, "Can you get him down, please?"

"He's okay," says Rashid.

"I'd like him to come down," says Brita. "Kyle, please get down."

"Um, well, I can't," says Kyle. "I'm going to stay here for a while."

"You'd better help him," Brita tells Rashid.

Miss Polly watches Rashid climb the tree. He shows Kyle where to put his feet. When Kyle is on the ground, Brita's shoulders relax.

"Sorry," says Rashid. "We were just exploring." He jumps to the ground.

Brita hugs Kyle then turns to Rashid, "I know it's easy for you to climb trees, but these boys are only five."

That's what happens when you let foreigners in your house, Miss Polly thinks.

"Maybe we can build a tree house *under* the tree," Rashid says.

"But then it's not a tree house!" Kyle complains.

"Of course, it is!" says Rashid. "It's an under-tree house."

"Okay," says Kyle.

"I like that idea very much," says Brita.

"We can call it 'Underwood,'" says

41

Teddy. He does not really want to climb the tree.

"Underwood," says Rashid. "Okay. Let's make a plan."

"Hmmph," says Miss Polly. She watches for a few more minutes. Brita goes inside, and Rashid sits on the grass with the boys.

Miss Polly leaves the window. She puts on her shoes and takes her dog for a walk. When they return, Tilly wants to sit in the sun, so Miss Polly leaves the door open. She goes inside, sits in her favorite chair, and closes her eyes.

Suddenly, Miss Polly wakes up. Someone is on her porch. She jumps up and sees Rashid. He is inside her front door, and Kyle is with him.

"Get out of my house! Get out! Get out!" Miss Polly yells.

Rashid holds up his hands, but she does not listen. "I'm calling the police," she says.

7. Winter Street

Kyle turns to run, but Rashid does not move. "Excuse me, ma'am. I'm happy to leave, but your dog just ran down the street."

Miss Polly's face changes. She looks for her dog. Tilly is not there.

"Tilly!" she yells. Miss Polly pushes past Rashid. She runs outside calling her dog's name. There are many cars and people on the street. A man is riding a bicycle, but there is no dog.

Miss Polly is old, but she walks fast. "Tilly!" She calls. Brita hears Miss Polly and comes outside with Ethan.

"Is Tilly your dog?" asks Brita, "The little black and white one?"

"Yes, that's Tilly!" says Miss Polly. "I left my door open, and she ran away."

"We can help," says Brita. She sees Rashid behind Miss Polly, and she takes charge. "Rashid, you and the boys go that way." She points toward Winter Street. "I'll call Dolores, and we'll go up Summer Street. Okay?"

Miss Polly nods. "I'll stay here."

Rashid and the boys are halfway down Winter Street when Teddy sees a small black and white dog. "There she is!" he says. Tilly disappears through a fence.

The boys run to the fence and stop. It is falling down, and so is the house behind it. The paint is coming off, and the windows are broken. There are dead

ALICE SAVAGE

plants in pots, and weeds are climbing
up the walls. Tilly is barking at something inside.

"Tilly," Rashid says. "Here doggie,
doggie."

Tilly looks at Rashid and barks. Then
she turns and jumps onto the porch.

"Stay here!" Rashid hands Kyle
his phone. "Call your mom," he says.
"Tell her we found Tilly." Kyle takes
the phone, but he forgets to call. He is
watching Rashid.

Rashid pulls himself up on the fence.
It starts to fall, but he jumps to the other
side. "Tilly," he calls. Tilly barks at
Rashid. Rashid gets down on his knees.
"Here doggie," he says in a quiet voice.
Tilly runs to him, and he picks her up.

He is trying to get back over the fence when Miss Polly arrives.

"I heard barking!" Miss Polly says. Then she sees her dog. "Tilly!"

Rashid hands the dog to Miss Polly.

Now Miss Polly is crying. "Don't ever do that again!" she says to her dog. Then she remembers Rashid. "Thank you!" she says.

Brita and Dolores come around the corner. Brita sees Miss Polly talking to Rashid. She is worried, but Miss Polly is smiling. "I yelled at him," Miss Polly points to Rashid. "He was trying to tell me about Tilly, and I yelled at him."

Rashid nods politely, but he is not listening. He and Kyle are looking over the fence at a strange sight. There is a long table under a tree. It has a dirty white tablecloth and broken plates.

"What are you looking at?" says Brita.

"That table. It looks like a party, but no one cleaned it up," says Rashid. "It's weird."

"It's scary," says Kyle looking at the broken windows and dead plants. "Does anyone live there?"

"No," says Miss Polly. "It's been like that forever."

"Do you know what happened?" asks Brita.

Miss Polly looks at Dolores. Dolores looks at Kyle and Teddy. Then she shakes her head. "Rashid's right. There was supposed to be a party, but it never happened. I'll get my husband to tell you the story some time when the kids are not around," she says quietly.

"Oh, I see," says Brita. She turns to Miss Polly. "I'm Brita."

"Oh, I'm sorry. I thought you knew each other," says Dolores. "I should have introduced you. This is Miss Polly."

"I live next door to you," says Miss Polly.

"I know," says Brita. "I've been meaning to introduce myself." She smiles. "I guess some good comes out of Tilly's little adventure."

"Thanks to you," says Miss Polly looking at Rashid. "Do you like dogs?"

"Of course," he says, turning to walk up the street. Miss Polly walks with him. Dolores and Brita follow with the boys. Brita smiles and points to the odd pair in front of them. Rashid is much taller than Miss Polly. He bends over to listen. Miss Polly is still carrying Tilly, and the dog looks back at them over her shoulder.

"Awww," says Dolores. "That's cute."

"It's the beginning of a beautiful friendship," says Brita.

8. A Long Night

Brita usually gives the boys a bath, and Joe usually reads them a story. Tonight is different. Joe is helping Rashid with paperwork. Rashid does not see the point. He does not have any money yet.

"You're going to need a bank account, and here's why," Joe begins.

Brita brings them peaches. Rashid told Brita he did not eat fruit during the war, so now she buys extra fruit. She sets out plates and knives so they can cut their fruit the Syrian way.

Next, she takes the boys upstairs to bed. She loves reading out loud, but after three books, Kyle still is not sleepy.

"I don't want to sleep with Ethan!" says Kyle.

"He's your brother," says Brita.

"I want my room," says Kyle.

"Why are you saying this now? Rashid is sleeping in your room," says Brita. "And Ethan likes having you here. Isn't that right, Ethan?" Ethan does not answer. He is already asleep.

"Can I sleep in your room?" asks Kyle.

"What is it, Kyle?"

"I can see the scary house," Kyle says.

Now Brita understands. Kyle's bed is next to a window, and his window is across from Winter Street. Brita can see the dirty white tablecloth through the trees. She covers the window.

Brita reads Kyle a story about a dog. The dog runs away. It gets very dirty. When the dog comes home, its family thinks it is a different dog. When the story is over, Kyle is still awake.

"You need to sleep," says Brita.

"Can you stay here? You can go when I am asleep."

"It's a deal," says Brita. She turns out the light and puts her arm around Kyle. He feels warm. She looks at him and smiles. Then she falls asleep, too.

Suddenly, a noise wakes Brita. She sits up and looks around. She is still in Ethan's room. Brita goes to the window. She hears a door close. She sees someone in the backyard. Then she sees a small orange light. She looks closer. Rashid is smoking a cigarette in her yard.

Brita feels nervous. She goes downstairs and looks out the front window.

Rashid is talking on the phone. He walks up and down the driveway. Then he opens the gate and walks down Summer Street.

Brita gets a drink of water and goes to her bedroom. Joe is sleeping, but now Brita cannot sleep. She thinks about Rashid. He is a nice kid, but he takes a lot of risks. *He is brave and strong*, she thinks. Kyle likes him, and Kyle is only five. What if Kyle follows Rashid and gets hurt?

Suddenly, her thoughts are interrupted by a loud noise. Joe sits up.

"It's coming from the other side of the house," he says. They run to Ethan's room and see Kyle at the window. "A fire!" Kyle says.

A house is burning on the next street.

Yellow and orange flames jump from the house. A tree catches on fire.

"That's Winter Street!" says Brita.

The lights of a fire truck flash in the distance. They hear the siren.

"A fire truck is coming," says Kyle excitedly. "Can we go see it?"

"No, honey. It's not safe," says Brita.

"Please! I want to see the fire truck!" he says. "Look! They're putting out the fire."

He is right. The firefighters work quickly, and soon the flames disappear. There is only the sound of water falling on the house.

Joe looks at the black shape of the house. "The fire *is* under control," he says. "I have to say, I'd like to see which house it is."

"I know which house it is," says Brita. "It's the house where we found Tilly. It's empty. Miss Polly said it's been empty for years."

"Then how did it catch on fire?" asks Joe.

"I want to see it!" says Kyle.

"But you don't like that house," says Brita.

"I want to see the fire truck!"

"I do, too," says Joe. "I promise. We'll be careful."

After they leave, Brita quietly opens the door to Rashid's bedroom and looks inside. His bed is empty. She closes the door and goes downstairs to make coffee. *Where is he?*

When Joe and Kyle return, Kyle is excited. "The truck is so big," he tells his mother. "And there's water everywhere. A tree fell on the party table. It's broken."

"Was anyone hurt?" Brita gives Joe a cup of coffee.

"It doesn't seem like it." Joe adds sugar and milk. "I talked to some neighbors, and they seemed happy to see it go."

"Do they know how it started?"

Joe shrugs. "No one knows. It's a mystery."

9. The River

The next day, Olivia leaves work early. She comes home to three hungry cats. She feeds them. Then she goes to her room and texts Keiko.

"That cute guy from across the street came to the shop!"

Keiko replies, "*And*?"

"I cut his hair." Olivia adds a smiley face.

Keiko sends a "thumbs up" emoji.

"There's more," Olivia replies.

"What?"

"We're going for a bike ride!"

Olivia puts down her phone and looks at two shirts on her bed. She tries on a blue shirt and takes a photo. Then she does the same with a white shirt.

She sends the photos to Keiko. Keiko thinks the white shirt looks best, but Olivia likes the blue one. It matches her eyes.

When she goes outside, Rashid is waiting. Olivia smiles. "Nice haircut."

"Thanks, I found a great stylist," Rashid says.

"Really?" says Olivia. She gets on her bike. "I need her number!"

"Yeah, but she's very busy. It's hard to get an appointment."

Rashid gets on Joe's bike, and they ride down Winter Street. When they pass the burned house, Rashid stops and pushes his sunglasses up. There is yellow police tape on the broken fence. Workers are taking out the wet, black wood and throwing it in a big truck.

Olivia points to pieces of the table and broken chairs.

"It's about time that got cleaned up," says Olivia. "It always scared me when I was a kid."

Rashid does not answer. He looks at the blackened house.

"Everything okay?" asks Olivia.

Rashid nods, saying "Just curious." He lowers his sunglasses over his eyes. "Lead the way."

Olivia takes Rashid on a bike path. It ends by a small river. Tall birds are standing in the water.

"This is beautiful," Rashid says. "What a great neighborhood!" He gets off his bike and stands next to her. "Have you lived here all your life?"

Olivia takes off her helmet and

shakes out her hair. "I'm afraid so."

"Why do you say that?" says Rashid. "This is a great place to grow up."

"My life is boring," says Olivia.

"Hmmm, I might not agree. I want to know you better before I decide."

Olivia sits on the grass. "I'm just a typical Houston kid. I went to schools in the neighborhood, and now I cut hair three blocks from my house. Someday I'll have adventures, but not just yet."

Rashid nods, "What kind of adventures?"

"I want to go to Greece."

"You'll like Greece," says Rashid. "There are cats everywhere."

"Really? Have you been there?"

"Briefly," says Rashid. "It wasn't really a vacation, though."

Olivia sits on the grass. "Your turn," she says. "I want to hear about you!"

Rashid sits next to her. "There's not much to tell. My life is boring, too."

"I don't think so," Olivia pauses. "I heard you were in a war."

Rashid does not want to talk about the war. "I'm going to be a doctor," he says. "That's pretty boring."

This surprises Olivia. "No, it's not. You have a goal!"

"It's a family goal," says Rashid.

"Oh?" says Olivia.

"My father was a doctor."

"I see."

"And his father was a doctor," says Rashid.

"Oh, right. I get it."

Rashid shows her a photo of his family. He points to his grandfather. The old man sits in a chair in the middle. On one side, she sees a tall man with glasses. He is wearing a hat. "My father," says Rashid. "And this is my mother on the other side."

Olivia looks closely. The woman is also tall like Rashid. She is wearing a scarf, and she has Rashid's dark eyes.

In the corner of the photo, two smiling boys stand a little bit apart.

"Which one is you?" asks Olivia, pointing to the boys.

Rashid points to the taller one.

"Is the other one your brother?"

"No, he's my best friend, Nabil," says Rashid. "I think he was at my house more than his own."

"Where is he now?" Olivia takes off her shoes.

"I'm not sure. He wants to bring his family to Germany, but his mother won't leave Syria."

"Why? Isn't she scared? How do they survive with all the bombing and stuff? How do they get food?"

"People find a way," says Rashid.

Olivia stops herself. "I'm sorry. I guess I can't imagine it."

"If they are in Aleppo, they have friends. Family and friends are everything in a war." Rashid picks up a rock and looks at it. "Nabil would do anything for his family. He'd do anything for me." Rashid throws the rock in the water. "I'd do anything for him."

Olivia thinks for a moment. "I don't know if my friend Keiko would do anything for me."

"She doesn't need to," says Rashid.

"What do you mean?"

"You're here. Life is easy." Rashid takes out his cigarettes. He looks at them. "I should quit," he says.

"You should. No one smokes anymore," says Olivia.

"I've noticed that." Rashid puts them away. "Sometimes I feel bad. Nabil's probably in danger, and I'm living a comfortable life in the US."

"Don't be hard on yourself," says Olivia. "You are doing good things. You've already rescued a dog."

Rashid smiles. "Thank you," he says. "Anyway, I'm going to start college this fall. Then I can help my family, and maybe Nabil."

"That makes sense," says Olivia.

"It makes me boring."

"There you go again!"

"Then let's agree that neither one of us is boring," says Rashid.

"Deal," says Oliva.

Rashid suddenly jumps up and kicks off his shoes. Then he holds out his hand. "This conversation is too serious for a beautiful girl on a summer day. Come on, let's go in the water!"

Olivia takes Rashid's hand. He pulls her up. They walk into the river. The fast water pushes against their legs, and Olivia falls. Rashid goes down with her. They jump up again, cold and wet, but laughing.

10. Arabic Music

A few days later, Rashid makes an announcement. He wants to cook Arabic food. Joe loves the idea, and so does Brita. They invite the neighbors for a Syrian meal, and on Saturday they go to the Arabic store.

Rashid invites Olivia, but she is giving her mother a haircut. Rashid says they can wait.

"Really?" says Brita. "The boys are already in the car."

"It's fine," says Joe. "It'll only take a few minutes. Let's have tea."

"You're so Syrian!" says Brita. She lets the boys out of the car, and they sit on the porch to wait for Olivia. Joe makes tea. They drink the sweet tea and watch squirrels run up and down the trees.

Finally, Olivia appears with her mother behind her. Brita waves, and the woman waves back. Brita starts to walk over to say hello, but Olivia's mother goes back in the house.

The Arabic store smells like spices and fresh bread. There are many families. Women in scarves put tea, rice, and vegetables in their shopping carts. The boys want fresh bread, so Brita takes them to the bakery.

Joe, Rashid, and Olivia look for meat. Olivia is surprised when she sees whole beef and lamb. The skinned animals hang from the ceiling, and men in white coats are taking them down and cutting off pieces. Joe and Rashid look at the meat and talk to the men in

Arabic. Finally, one man takes down a lamb. He cuts a large piece and puts it in white paper.

Next, Rashid puts spices, vegetables, and rice in the cart. Joe throws in some tea. Brita appears with bread and cookies for the boys. Olivia buys chocolate.

When they return, Rashid takes charge of the kitchen.

"I'll help him," Joe tells Brita. "You rest."

Rashid turns on Arabic music. He starts to dance. Then Joe joins him. They are holding wooden spoons and laughing.

Olivia takes a photo.

Suddenly, the water boils over. It makes a noise when it hits the fire. "Watch out!" yells Brita. She jumps up.

Rashid stops her. "I've got this," he says. "My mom taught me." He lights the stove again.

Brita disagrees, but Ethan wakes up from a nap and cries. Brita brings him downstairs. "I'm going to take Ethan outside," she says.

"What?" asks Joe. The music is loud.

Brita does not answer. She is already outside with Ethan. It is hot outside, but at least it is quiet.

After a few minutes, Joe opens the door. He sees Brita and Ethan. They are lying on the grass and looking up into the tree.

Joe comes outside. "There you are," he says. "Everything okay?"

"Fine," says Brita.

Joe sits on the steps. "Are you sure?"

Brita nods, "I just need a little quiet time."

Ethan walks toward the steps. Brita stands up to help him. She takes Ethan's hand and holds him steady while he climbs up.

"How about a walk?" asks Joe. "We haven't talked in a while."

"You've been busy," says Brita.

"I know, the shop."

"And Rashid."

"And Rashid." Joe puts Ethan on his shoulders. They walk down Summer Street. The trees move in the light wind. Ethan reaches up to touch the leaves.

"It's good to see you having fun," Brita says. "You seem younger with Rashid."

"Yes. He connects me with my past," Joe says. "I've forgotten so much."

"That's good, I guess," says Brita.

"Still, I know this isn't easy for you," says Joe. "How are you doing?"

"I guess I *am* a little stressed," Brita says.

"Yeah, I thought this might happen."

"I like Rashid." Brita pauses.

"But?" asks Joe.

"Sometimes I feel like things are out of control. He had Kyle up in a tree."

"Kyle is a boy. He might climb trees anyway."

"Yes, but maybe not so soon. And Rashid smokes."

"I know," says Joe. "He's trying to quit."

"There's something else," says Brita.

She tells Joe about seeing Rashid on the night of the fire. "I don't want to suggest that he did it," she says. "But I thought you should know."

11. A Fall

Rashid and Olivia set up a table in the yard. They cover it with a white cloth and bring out plates and glasses. There are flowers from Dolores's yard.

"It's beautiful," says Brita. She remembers the other table. It was under the broken-down house on Winter Street. *What happened to that family?*

Suddenly a scream comes from behind the house. There is a sound like something hitting the ground. Then a yell.

Everyone stops. Rashid is the first to move. He runs out the gate and around the corner.

"It's on Winter Street," says Olivia.

"Stay here with the kids," says Brita.

Then she and Joe run after Rashid. When they arrive, he is on the ground next to one of the workers. The worker is white with pain. He has blood on his shirt, and his arm looks strange.

Joe takes out his phone. "I'll call for help," he says.

The hurt worker shakes his head, "No!" he says. He looks afraid. "Don't call!"

Rashid looks at the man. "I can help," he says. Then he feels the worker's arm and shoulder. The worker looks at him. His eyes are big and afraid.

"It's not broken," Rashid says. He helps the worker stand up. Then Rashid holds the man's shoulder and pulls his arm. The man yells again. Then he stops. He feels better.

"Aren't you going to call 911?" Brita asks Joe.

"No," says the worker. "Please. No doctor."

Brita is confused.

"He's going to be okay," says Rashid.

Joe puts away his phone.

Someone gives the man a drink. The other workers stand around Rashid. They smile and pat him on the shoulder. Rashid looks at the cut on the man's arm. "It's not serious," he says, "but you need to clean it."

The men take the worker away in a truck.

Brita looks at Rashid. "I can't believe you did that!"

Rashid shrugs. "He dislocated his shoulder. I put it back."

Brita shakes her head. "That was dangerous, Rashid."

Rashid is surprised. "You think I did something wrong?"

"No, but in this country, we call 911," says Brita. "We have trained medics. It's better to let them deal with accidents."

Rashid frowns. "If I see a person in pain, you want me to wait for the medics?"

"Well," says Brita. "What I mean is … you don't want to make things worse. You could get in trouble."

"I'm sorry, but I don't agree with you," says Rashid.

"I know you want to help," says Brita, "but—"

"Yes, and I *will* help," says Rashid, "If something is wrong, I can't walk away.

That's who I am." He turns and goes back up the street.

Brita watches Rashid turn the corner. "What just happened?" she asks Joe.

Joe tries to explain. "Rashid comes from a different world."

"The war," Brita sighs. "You tried to tell me."

"Yes," says Joe. "Remember that he came here with nothing. Just one suitcase. He's lost so much. His father. His country. His friends. There's one thing he'll never give up."

"What's that?"

"His honor."

12. A Party

When Joe and Brita get home, Dolores and her husband Paco are talking to Rashid on the porch. Rashid looks quickly at Brita. "Look who's here," he says. "You visit. I need to check on the food." He goes inside.

Dolores introduces Paco, and Joe likes him immediately. Paco is short and round. He has a friendly face. "I hear you built a tree house, but on the ground," Paco says. "That's smart!"

"It's called 'Underwood,'" says Joe. "Come on, I'll show you." He takes Paco to the backyard. They stop in front of a small wooden house under a big tree. Inside there is room for two small chairs and a table.

ALICE SAVAGE

"Did the boys build this?" Paco asks.

"Rashid helped a little."

Paco walks around the house and brushes some leaves off. Then he steps back. "Not bad," he says.

"They want to paint it." Joe points to some paint cans.

"That sounds like fun," says Paco. "I'd like to help."

Joe laughs, "I'm glad to hear it. Are you free next weekend?"

"Yes," says Paco. He gets down on his hands and knees. He already has ideas. "We could make a sign for the front: UNDERWOOD." Then he corrects himself. "I mean *the boys* could make a sign."

The two men talk about different

possibilities for Underwood. Then they go through the house to get drinks.

In the kitchen, Miss Polly is talking to Brita and Dolores. "What is Rashid making?" she asks. "Is it weird?"

"He's cooking lamb's head," says Dolores. She moves so Paco and Joe can come in. Now everyone is in the kitchen.

"I'm not going to eat lamb's head," says Miss Polly.

"It's a joke, Miss Polly," says Dolores.

Olivia laughs, "I watched them buy it, Miss Polly. It's the leg. I promise."

Miss Polly is not sure she believes Olivia, but she wants to stay. If she does not like Rashid's dinner, she will go home and open a can of soup. She looks at the pot on the stove. It smells unusual, but it looks delicious.

Rashid tastes the food and adds a little salt. Then he puts rice on a big plate. He uses napkins to pick up the hot stew pot.

"Ready!" he says. Paco holds the door for Rashid. Olivia follows with rice. Then Dolores comes with green vegetables. Brita and Miss Polly bring bread. Joe has drinks. They watch Rashid put the lamb stew on the table. "Sit," he says. Everyone finds a place.

Dolores takes out her camera. "Say cheese!" she says.

"Cheese!" everyone but Brita looks up and smiles.

"Brita?" says Dolores.

"What?"

"Smile!"

"Oh, sorry," Brita smiles, and Dolores takes the photo.

"Now let's eat!" says Rashid. He puts rice and stew on a plate and gives it to Miss Polly.

"I can't eat all that," she says.

"Sure, you can," Rashid continues to serve. Soon everyone has a big plate of food. Kyle and Teddy take their food to the tree house. The adults sit around the table and talk. The sun is low in the sky. Light shines through the branches of a leafy tree, and they can hear birds.

While they eat, Joe asks Paco about the scary house. "What do you know about that old house on Winter Street? The one that burned down?"

"Oh, that's a terrible story! Are you sure you want to hear it?"

"Yes!" says everyone at once.

"Okay, but it doesn't have a happy ending," says Paco.

13. Two Houses

"The house on Winter Street was one of the first houses in the neighborhood. It was built about 100 years ago," says Paco. "It belonged to one family, the Grahams. The last owner was Fred Graham. He was a history professor, and he and his wife Shirley lived there a long time. They had one child, a boy named Dirk. He was a weird kid. I didn't know him well. He left right after high school."

"Sad," says Dolores.

"I'd say lucky," says Miss Polly.

Paco continues, "I don't know how the Grahams felt, but they were already old when Dirk left. Shirley was sick, and Fred took care of her."

Paco takes a drink and leans forward.

"Then a strange thing happened. Shirley's brother and his wife moved in. They brought their children, too. They said they wanted to help take care of Shirley."

"But they actually wanted a free place to live," says Miss Polly. "Isn't that true, Paco?"

"Well, that's what we think because of what happened later."

"What happened?" asks Brita.

"Well, first I need to tell you about these relatives. They liked parties, and Fred wasn't happy about it. I heard fighting, especially in the summer when all the windows were open. One night, I was in the backyard, and I heard a siren. My father came in and told me to stay inside. He said the police were there."

"Uh, oh," says Olivia. "The old man killed his relatives."

Rashid looks at Olivia. "People don't kill their families."

"Actually, he did," says Paco. "Fred Graham killed his family."

"Seriously?" Joe sets down his glass.

"How?" asks Brita.

"Poison. It was in their drinks."

"That's terrible!" says Rashid.

"Well, they wouldn't leave, and he wanted his house back. He was really angry, I guess."

"Obviously!" says Miss Polly.

"Did he poison his wife, too?" asks Rashid.

"He killed everyone in the house," says Paco. "Even himself. When the party guests arrived, the whole family was on the floor, dead."

"No wonder the kid doesn't come back," says Dolores.

"So that table …" says Brita.

"Yep, that table was set for a party that never happened."

Everyone is silent for a minute. They are thinking about the table with the dirty white cloth.

Rashid is staring at Paco. "Wow! That guy really didn't like relatives!"

"No, some families just can't get along," says Paco.

14. The Truth

"The fire was a good thing if you ask me," says Miss Polly. "That house needed to go."

"So, Paco, do you know *how* the house caught on fire?" asks Brita.

"No, I haven't heard anything," says Paco.

"Yeah, about that …" says Rashid.

Now everyone looks at Rashid.

"Do you know something about the fire, Rashid?" asks Brita.

"Well, yeah, I guess I need to tell you something."

"What?" asks Joe.

"I was there that night. I was walking by, and I saw some homeless people inside."

"What were they doing?" asks Paco.

"I think they were just talking, but one of them asked me for a cigarette."

"Did you give it to him?" asks Brita.

"Yeah. He was friendly. We talked about the weather."

"You talked about the weather with a homeless man?" asks Miss Polly.

"Yeah, why not? I gave him a light and then moved on."

Brita shakes her head, "Oh, Rashid! I wish you had told me because I saw you!"

Everyone looks at Rashid.

"But I didn't start the fire," he says.

Brita sighs. "I saw you leave, and the next thing I knew, a house burned down."

"It wasn't me!" says Rashid.

"I believe you, but I didn't know then."

Rashid looks down. "You don't trust me."

"Give me time," says Brita. "It's a big change."

Everyone gets quiet.

"No, I should leave," Rashid says.

Brita shakes her head.

"It's fine, Rashid says. "I'll find another place to live. I'll get a job."

"No," Brita says. "I want you to stay."

Brita looks at Joe. "My husband enjoys having you here. He's been happy."

Rashid looks at Joe and back at Brita, "Yeah, but—"

"Let me finish," Brita says. "The boys like you, too."

"Heck, I like him," says Miss Polly. "And that's saying a lot!"

Everyone laughs nervously.

Brita continues, "And I like you, too! Really, I do."

Rashid's shoulders relax, "Are you sure?" he says.

"Yes. It'll be fine because ..." Brita looks at the table full of food, "you can cook!" She smiles.

Rashid gets the joke. "Okay, then. But one more thing. If you change your mind, don't poison me."

Brita laughs, "No, I promise. I won't poison you. We do things a little differently in this family."

"I won't poison you either." Rashid puts his hand over his heart.

"I'm glad to hear it," says Brita.

"Then why aren't you eating?" Rashid puts a napkin over his hair. He looks like a woman in a scarf. "My mother isn't here, so I have to take her place." Then in a high woman's voice, he says, "You need to eat your vegetables!"

Brita laughs and lets Rashid put more food on her plate.

When the meal is over, they drink tea and continue talking. It is dark now, but a string of lights shines a soft yellow on the small group sitting around the table. Miss Polly talks about inviting her relatives to visit. "Rashid, it's because of you," she says.

"Me?"

"Yes, I think I'll invite my niece to live with me. Then she can go to university here, too."

"That's a great idea," says Olivia, "I'm going to college, too, but first I want to travel." She looks at Rashid. "I always wanted to, but now it seems possible."

"See! You've changed us all in different ways," says Brita.

"I didn't mean to," says Rashid

"But they're good ways!" says Olivia.

"Olivia's right," says Brita. "And now that we have everything worked out, life should calm down."

At that moment, Joe's phone lights up. He picks it up. "Keep talking," he says. "I need to take this." Then he stands up and walks to the fence.

Brita watches him. She knows that walk. He is talking to someone in Jordan. Rashid is also quiet. Brita and

Rashid share a look. Whatever Joe is talking about, it is important.

Joe talks for a long time. Then he hangs up and comes back to the table.

"Well?" says Brita. She is trying to see if Joe has good news or bad, but she cannot tell.

"It's Rashid's mother," Joe says. "Mona just got her paperwork in order, and she's coming to Texas."